The Littl

RODIN

Catherine de Duve

FOR EVERYONE !

Find out about the life and work
of the famous French sculptor

KATE'ART
EDITIONS

Rodin, the thinker?

Rodin, father of modern sculpture!
In Rodin's day, sculpture is supposed to perfectly reflect reality (by convention and in the academic tradition). Rodin imagines a new way of working which is free and very expressive. Will the public understand and appreciate him?

Rodin's originality
Rodin reinvents sculpture. He takes apart his plaster models, separating them into legs, arms, hands, torso and head. He then reassembles these fragments into a new body. Why not put one person's head with another person's hand? It creates surprising effects!

Inspired by the old masters
Although Rodin breaks with the artistic criteria of his day, he draws inspiration from the old masters. Like Michelangelo, Rodin paints and sculpts powerful, monumental figures.

The Hôtel Biron

A house of artists

In 1905, the Hôtel Biron, named after its first owner the Duke of Biron, in *rue de Varenne* in Paris, is rented out to young artists: the poet Jean Cocteau, the painter Henri Matisse, the American dancer Isadora Duncan...

'The Charmettes de Paris'

In 1908, Rodin rents four large, connected rooms. He covers the walls with his drawings and fills the rooms with his large art collection and his own sculptures. His friends come to listen to his gramophone. The house is soon put up for sale and only Rodin can stay. After his death, the sculptor leaves his art to the State, and, in 1909, the Hôtel Biron becomes the Rodin Museum.

In Rodin's workshop

**In the workshop,
everyone has a job to do.**

Auguste Rodin is sitting holding
a notebook. The master is
supervising the work of his pupils
and assistants. Who are they?

The '**metteur au point**' cuts the
marble block down to the size of
the model. Then the '**practiciens**',
professional carvers, sculpt
the marble into its exact shape.
Rodin works with talented
sculptors such as Bourdelle,
Pompon, Claudel...

Materials and Techniques

Clay modelling
The sculptor uses clay to produce a model. He kneads the clay vigorously in his hands and looks at his subject from all angles. He creates the shape by adding or taking away small lumps of clay. This study will then be used to create a plaster cast or a marble sculpture.

Plaster mould
Initially, the plaster cast is used to create a mould, so the original shape can be reproduced in another material (bronze). The mould also allows the sculptor to create a whole series of the same sculpture. Rodin is different, though: the plaster cast itself becomes an artwork, and no longer just a mould! This is his favourite form of expression.

Marble
Marble, used since ancient times by the Greeks and then the Romans because of its whiteness and hardness, is the most valuable material used by sculptors. Carving it is extremely difficult and risky because of its veins, which can lead to sudden splitting of the block. It takes a lot of skill.

Bronze
Bronze is a metal (a copper and tin alloy). The moulder makes a model (the core) which is covered in wax, and then creates a plaster mould. The bronze is cast in a foundry at a temperature of 10,500 degrees C. The wax melts, runs out through pipes, and is replaced by the bronze.

Auguste Rodin

Auguste Rodin is born on 12 November 1840 in Paris. The Rodins are not well-off. They live in a poor district of town. Rodin's father works at the police department and his mother cannot read or write.

Drawing

Auguste loves drawing! He copies pictures on grocery packages. His big sister encourages him. He leaves Paris to lodge with his uncle in Beauvais. He's bored there, but he visits the gothic cathedral, the biggest in France, which he finds impressive.

Ink blots

Rodin is short-sighted, and has a vivid imagination. He looks at ink blots and can see stars and people. Later, he makes quick drawings on scraps of paper. His models don't pose, but wander freely around his studio.

Often Rodin draws without looking at the paper. His art is spontaneous and lively!

Apprenticeship

The 'Little School'

Rodin wants to be an artist! His parents agree, if he becomes the best! At the age of 14, he starts at the 'Little School', the Imperial School of Design and Mathematics (which would later become the School of Decorative Arts) in Paris.

At the Louvre museum

Every afternoon, Auguste visits museums and copies works by the old masters. He also draws them from memory. In the evening, he attends life drawing classes at the Manufacture des Gobelins. He is very good at modelling and drawing, but how can he become a famous artist?

Failure

Rodin takes the entry exam for the School of Fine Art but fails three times.

Priest

In 1862, Auguste, devastated by the death of his sister Maria, joins the Congregation of the Blessed Sacrament as a novice. There, Father Eymard encourages him to carry on sculpting. Rodin makes a sculpture of him, but the priest thinks he looks devilish, with his curly hair like horns! Sculptors at the time don't do this: they are supposed to idealise their model, not the opposite…

Sculptor-ornamentalist

At the time, Paris is a huge building-site (Haussmann's development work). Paris is being beautified! The craftsmen in the school produce ornamental pieces to decorate squares and buildings. It's a growth business! Rodin joins Carrier-Belleuse's workshop, making decorative objects (for the Paris Opera etc.). There he learns about mass production. Auguste meets a young seamstress, Rose Beuret, who becomes his partner.

Bibi, his first model

The young Rodin can't afford to pay a model. The man who looks after the horses at the market comes and poses in his studio. He has a lined face, rough skin, a broken, boxer's nose, and bristly eyebrows. Rodin doesn't idealise his face.

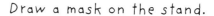
Draw a mask on the stand.

The accident

It's winter, it's very cold in the studio. Bibi's head, modelled in clay, freezes and breaks off. All that is left is a mask (the front of the face). Rodin decides that this will be his finished work. He presents Bibi, the *Man with a Broken Nose*, to the 1865 Salon. Unfortunately, it is rejected, as the jury sees it as a 'fragment of sculpture'. Only ten years later will Bibi finally be exhibited at the Salon.

The Walking Man

First 'assemblage'

Rodin reuses a sculpture of Saint John the Baptist.
He enlarges it so it's larger than life. He moulds the
torso, which he bends forward slightly, and removes
the head and arms. The man looks as if he's walking
energetically. The artist suggests the most important
things: movement and life. Nothing else matters much!

 Compare *Saint John the Baptist* with the *Walking Man*.
Which of his legs is longer?

1880

1907

9

The Franco-Prussian War

In 1870, Rodin is 30. He is called up as a corporal in the National Guard, but is then discharged because of his short-sightedness.

Brussels

At the time of the siege of Paris, Rodin joins Carrier-Belleuse in Brussels and stays there for six years. There is work, and Rose joins him. Rodin teams up with the Belgian sculptor Van Rasbourgh and works, in particular, on the décor of the Palais des Académies, the Stock Exchange and the Brussels Conservatory.

Rodin the painter

Rodin visits Belgian museums and cities, but really likes going for long walks in the woods with Rose. The artist paints a series of small landscapes of the Forest of Soignes, near Brussels.

Look at these landscapes, painted from nature. Where would you like to walk?

Italy, a study trip

At the age of 35, Auguste Rodin, like many artists, travels to Italy to study art there. He discovers the work of Italian Renaissance artists such as Michelangelo, who inspires him.

Try and pose like these two statues. Do the poses feel natural? What does Rodin's figure have in his hand: a sword, lance, flame or fishing-rod?

Scandal!

Rodin creates his first important work in Brussels. *The Age of Bronze*, created firstly in plaster, is a perfect life-size figure of a young man. The sculpture is exhibited in Brussels (1877) then in Paris. It's so realistic that Rodin is accused of casting it on a real body. Rodin has to defend himself and prove the opposite. What skilful work!

Success

It's an immediate success! Rodin receives many commissions for portraits. He finally achieves recognition, and, in 1880, the French State buys the sculpture from him.

11

The Gates of Hell

Monument
Rodin is 40 when he receives his first official State commission. He designs the extravagant *Gates of Hell*, a monument intended as the entry to the future Decorative Arts Museum in Paris. The museum is never built, but Rodin continues to work 'furiously' on hundreds of figures for it. The gateway becomes his laboratory.

Dante Alighieri
Rodin chooses to illustrate the poem *The Divine Comedy* by the Italian poet Dante Alighieri (1265-1321). In this, the poet is led by Virgil to the centre of the earth, and discovers the damned in hell.

Composition & **Expression** & Passion
More and more figures are added to the doorway. They float, stand, fall, twist into strange shapes, clutch at each other or grimace in despair in waves of lava. The bodies are modelled very expressively.

Look at the plaster version of *The Gates*, created between 1880 and 1917.

A source of shapes
Rodin sets the figures free from the gateway itself. He enlarges some (*The Kiss*, *The Thinker*, etc.). The unfinished plaster gateway is shown to the public at Rodin's first individual exhibit, during the 1900 Universal Exhibition.

e gateway weighs
tons. It took 55
conds to cast!

The gateway features more
than 200 groups and figures.
Find *The Three Shades*
and *The Thinker*.

Tympanum

Lintel

Door

Pilaster

Fugit Amor

Bas-relief

The Three Shades

These three figures represent ghosts of the dead, now only shadows. They are the guardians of *The Gates of Hell*.

Interesting fact
This group is made up of three identical casts of the same figure. Two of them have had an arm removed and have been placed in different positions – you can see the family likeness!

Scoop
Rodin is the first sculptor to break up his artworks, just like ancient statues which, even with a broken or damaged limb, are still beautiful. Was he inspired by antique sculptures?

Abandon hope, all ye who enter here!

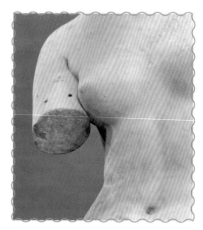

The Venus de Milo *is an ancient Greek sculpture (ca. 130-100 B.C.). It has no arms, but retains its mysterious beauty.*

UGOLINO

Horror!

The legend tells that, in the 13th century, Count Ugolino, the tyrannical ruler of Pisa, was imprisoned in a tower for betraying the Emperor, who was himself fighting against the Pope. Driven mad by hunger, he devoured his dead children and was condemned to hell. Here he is naked, gaping and crawling along like a scavenger. He has lost his humanity. His humiliating pose is shocking. What a dreadful story!

Technique

Each limb of the body is cast separately. The various parts are then assembled on a stand using material soaked in plaster, to form a static figure. There you are – a new group sculpture!

Other artists before Rodin illustrated this horrific story. Compare the two styles. Which do you find most expressive?

Auguste Rodin, 1881   Jean-Baptiste Carpeaux, 1861

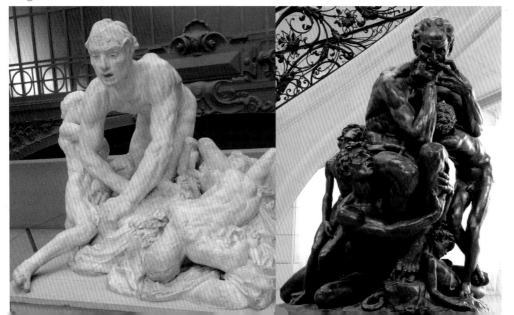

In 1883, Rodin meets the talented Camille Claudel (1864-1943).
She's 19, he's 43. She becomes his assistant, co-worker and muse. Rodin portrays her in his sculptures. They are very much in love and work passionately together for many years, but in the end they separate. Claudel is devastated by the break-up and loses her mind. She destroys many of her works and remains locked up until her death.

Assemblage
Camille's head and Pierre de Wissant's hand (*Burghers of Calais*). What does that make?

What a contrast!
Camille is wearing a Breton cap. Her head emerges from a large block of rough marble which emphasises the features of her delicately polished muse's face.

16

Claudel comes to Paris to take art classes. The Fine Arts School is not then open to women, so she joins the *Académie de la Grande Chaumière* and rents a studio where the sculptor Alfred Boucher, a friend of her father's, comes to teach. Boucher leaves for Rome and is replaced by Rodin. Claudel soon joins his workshop in rue de l'Université.

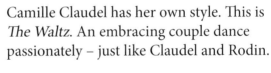

Mademoiselle Claudel has become my most outstanding worker, I consult her on everything.

Camille Claudel has her own style. This is *The Waltz*. An embracing couple dance passionately – just like Claudel and Rodin.

Brilliant Camille!
The young girl's work is exceptional! It leaves a 'strong impression' on Rodin. She sculpts a bust of him in his own style.

17

The Burghers of Calais

In 1884, the town of Calais commissions Rodin to create a monument commemorating a striking episode in the Hundred Years' War.

The story of the burghers of Calais

In 1347, having laid siege to the town of Calais, Edward III of England, impressed by the courage of the townspeople, offers to spare them on one condition: six eminent figures must volunteer to hand the key of the town over to him and then be hanged.

Slowly, the six heroes advance side by side, without touching. They are barefoot and clothed in a simple tunic, with ropes around their necks. Spot the key to the town and the ropes.

The sculptures are often coated with a patina of acid. This makes them look 'worn'. Find the traces of this.

12 of these sculptures were made in bronze. They can be seen in several places, including Calais, Basel, Paris (on the left), London, Copenhagen, New York, Seoul and Tokyo (below).

The Kiss

The lovers' story

Gianciotto, Francesca's husband, has gone off to war. While he is away, his wife falls in love with her brother-in-law, Paolo. They are reading the adventures of Lancelot together and kiss. Surprised by the husband/brother, the two lovers are killed and condemned to hell.

Rodin portrays a happy and universal moment. He enlarges his marble model. He works on it with Claudel. It's an immediate success. The public calls it *The Kiss*. Everyone wants their own copy! Rodin reproduces miniature versions of the sculpture.

Compare the 3 materials: find the bronze, the marble and the terracotta.
Spot the hand which is out of proportion compared to the body.

Which do you prefer, marble or bronze?
Which substance is stronger?

  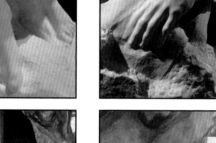

 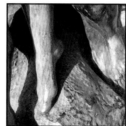 

Treasure hunt at the Musée Rodin!

Find the miniature bronze versions of *Thinker* and *Fugit amor*.

Monet

22 September 1897

My dear Monet,

I was so pleased to receive your letter [...] The same brotherly feelings, the same love of art, have made us friends forever [...] I still have the same admiration for the artist who helped me understand light, the clou the sea, the cathedrals which I already loved so much, but the beauty of which you showed me in a new, dau light, which touched me deeply.

Rodin

SCOOP

Rodin and Monet* are born nearly on the same day, in the same city. They admire each other. In 1889, they exhibit together in the Georges Petit gallery in Paris.

Monet gives Rodin a picture. What does Rodin's letter to his friend tell us about this impressionist picture? Both artists create series of artworks: Monet produces series of haystacks, the sea and cathedrals.

* To find out more, take a look at *The Little Monet.*

Mount Fuji

This young girl's body is like a sculpture. How beautiful!

Kimono

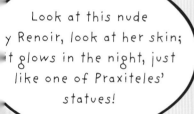

Collector

Around 1893, Rodin starts to collect Roman sculptures, Greek vases and Egyptian figurines. He ends up with more than 6,000 filling his home.

Rodin also likes fashionable Japanese prints, and acquires paintings by Van Gogh and Renoir.

Look at this nude y Renoir, look at her skin; t glows in the night, just like one of Praxiteles' statues!

Where am I on show in Mr Rodin's house?

Balzac

Rodin is successful, very successful!
He receives commissions for a sculpture
of Victor Hugo (for the Pantheon), Balzac
(for the Luxembourg Gardens) and
Claude Lorrain (for the city of Nancy).

Balzac in a dressing gown

Rodin does some research about Balzac. He looks
at photographs, paintings and sculptures showing
the writer, who died in 1850. He immerses himself
in Balzac's world, reads his books, visits his home-region,
questions people who knew him, like his tailor.
What was Balzac like as a person?

A revolutionary portrait

Rodin gets down to work. He finds a model
who could pass for Balzac and makes many clay
studies. After six long years, here is a portrait
showing the power of Balzac's genius rather
than his physical appearance.

Scandal!

The sculpture is too innovative for its time,
and the commission is cancelled. Rodin is
too modern, and is not yet understood.

*He doesn't need props, a book or a writer's
pen. His powerful presence is enough. Like
a colossus, Balzac, his head held high, defies
the world. His body seems to be carved from
one block. His head and hair are unkempt.
You can sense the man rather than see him.*

Dressing gown

This is the monk's habit that Balzac wore
to write in. To sculpt the drapery, Rodin
dresses his model in a wrap-around dressing
gown. He coats it in plaster to stiffen it.
He then uses this gown to produce his mould.
The sculpture is cast later, in 1935.

Non finito

Rodin considers this plaster
as a finished work, although
it has neither head nor hands.
Over to you now! Draw in
the missing parts of the body.
What an interesting effect!

Here is an enlarged version of *The Thinker* (the poet Dante of *The Gates of Hell*), created by Rodin in 1880. Deep in thought, this athlete at rest embodies mental and physical strength.

Just like Rodin, sketch *the Thinker*, showing volume (shadows and highlights).

Danaid

The myth of the Danaids

The daughters of Danaos, the Danaids, were made to eternally fill up a bottomless jar with water, as punishment for killing their husbands on their wedding night.

Exhausted

Rodin chooses to show not the jar, but the feelings of exhaustion and despair at having to constantly re-begin this pointless task. This graceful figure is one of the Danaids. Her back and neck are facing the light. Her smooth, transparent skin shines on the polished marble, while beneath her, the marble block is carved roughly and shows tool-marks. Her hair merges with the water running out of an invisible jar, like a long sob. Can you hear it?

 Compare the plaster version of *Danaid* to the marble version. What differences can you see? Which do you prefer?

GUSTAV KLIMT

Like Rodin, Klimt (1862–1918) portrays a passage from the myth of the Danaids. Compare the 2 versions. Do you prefer Rodin's sculpture (1889) or Klimt's painting (1907)?

Portraits

> A man very rarely sees himself as he really is!

Rodin has become famous. He produces
many portraits of famous and wealthy people.

Sitting for the sculptor

While everyone in Paris wants a portrait by the great master, they don't like
posing for hours during the many sessions needed to produce a bust.
Victor Hugo refuses to pose, and Rodin has to follow him around
his house. It can't be easy to observe and model clay at the same time!

Many customers aren't satisfied: Rodin doesn't make them look good, but shows
them as he sees them.

Find the names of the people sculpted here: Bibi, Rose,
Balzac, Hugo, Claudel, Carrier-Belleuse.
Do you recognize them?

Meudon

Rodin moves to Meudon to the *Villa des Brillants*. There he welcomes visiting friends, artists and writers like the Austrian poet Rilke.

The First World War breaks out. On 29 January 1917, Rodin marries Rose, his first companion, who dies on 14 February. Auguste Rodin dies a few months later, on 17 November 1917, at the age of 77. He is buried in his garden in Meudon, beside Rose. Over their tombs is the sculpture *The Thinker*.

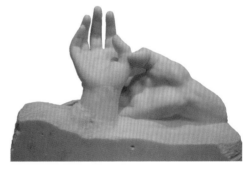

Rodin hands over to the young artists he has inspired!

Text: Catherine de Duve
Concept and editorial coordination: Kate'Art Editions
Layout: Julie Brousmiche

PHOTOGRAPHIC CREDITS:

Rodin:

Paris: Musée Rodin: *Danaid* (marble), 1889: cover, p.1, p.28, *Mask of Camille Claudel and left hand of Pierre de Wissant* (plaster), ca. 1895: p.2, p.16, *Study for the head of Balzac* (terracotta), 1891: p.2, p.25, *Figure drawing of a naked man, seen from behind*, 1870: p.2, *Despair*, 1893: p.3, *The Cathedral* (marble), 1908: p.5, *The Cathedral* (plaster) 1908: p.2, p.5, *Male nude known as Nude study B for Balzac*, ca. 1891: p.5, *Naked woman with veil*, 1890: p.6, *Intertwined couple or the circle of loves*, 1880-1886: p.6, *Father Eymard* (bronze), ca.1863: p.7, *Rose Beuret*, 1865: p.8, *Albert-Ernest Carrier-Belleuse* (bronze), 1882: p.8, p.30, *Man with a broken nose* (bronze), 1864: p.8, *Saint John the Baptist*, 1880 (bronze): p.9, *The Walking man* (bronze), 1907: p.9, *Red houses near Boitsfort*, 1871-1877: p.10, *Dirt track to Watermael through the Forest of Soignes*, 1871-1877: p.10, *Barges. On the bank of the canal at Willebroek*, 1871-1877: p.10, *The Age of bronze* (bronze), 1877: p.11, *The Three Shades* (bronze), ca.1904: p.14, *Thought* (marble), 1890: p.16, *Camille Claudel with a bonnet*, ca.1884: p.16, *The Kiss* (terracotta), ca.1881: p.20, *The Kiss* (marble), ca. 1881: p.20, p.21, *Monument to the Burghers of Calais* (bronze), ca. 1885-1895: p.16, p.18, p.19, *Man with a broken nose* (marble), 1864: p.30, *Camille Claudel with short hair*, ca.1882: p.30, *Head of Balzac, penultimate study*, ca.1896-1897: p.25, *Balzac, study for the dressing gown*, 1897 (plaster): p.25, *Danaid* (plaster), 1889: p.28, *Lovers' hands*, 1904, *Rodin's Signature* (bronze): p.31

Musée de l'Orangerie: *The Kiss* (bronze), ca.1881: p.20

Musée d'Orsay: *The Walking Man*, 1907: p.2, p. *The Gates of Hell* (plaster), ca.1889-1890: p.12, *Ugolino*, 1881: p.15, *Danaid* (plaster), ca.1889: p.28, *Victor Hugo* (bronze), 1897: p.30

Angers: Musée des beaux-arts: *Rose Beuret en Mignon*, 1870: p.30

Helsinki: Ateneum: Allan Österlind: *Rodin in his studio*, 1885: p.3

Private collection: *The Cathedral* (bronze), 1908, *The Thinker*, 1903: cover

Tokyo: National Museum of Western Art: *Adam* (bronze), 1880-1881: cover, *Eve* (bronze), 1881: cover, *The Gates of Hell* (bronze), ca.1889-1890: pp. 12-13, *Monument to the Burghers of Calais* (bronze), ca. 1885-1895: p.19, *The Thinker* (bronze), 1903: p.27, p.31,

Hakone: Open Air Museum: *Monument to Balzac* (bronze), 1898: p.24

Paris: Musée du Louvre: *Venus de Milo*, ca. 130-100 B.C.: p.15, Musée d'Orsay: **Carpeaux:** *Ugolino*, 1861: p.15, Musée Rodin: **Avigdor:** *Rodin in his studio*, 1897-1898: p. 6, **Claudel:** *Bust of Rodin*, 1892: p.17, *The Waltz*, 1989-1890: p.17, **Monet:** Paris: Musée Rodin: *Belle-île*, 1886, **Van Gogh:** *Portrait of Père Tanguy*, 1887: p.23, **Renoir:** *Female nude*, ca. 1880, Hans Dichand Collection: **Klimt:** *Danae*, 1907, Florence: Galleria dell'Accademia: **Michelangelo:** *David*, 1501-1504: p.11, **Praxiteles:** Glyptothek, Munich: *Aphrodite Braschi*, ca.370-330 B.C.: p.23

Photographs: P. Dornac, *Rodin in front of the Monument to Sarmiento, Hands in pockets, Tools placed on a plank of wood*, 1898: cover, p.1, p.22, *Camille Claudel*, before 1883: p.16, W.Elborne, *Camille Claudel and Jessie Lipscomb in their studio, 117 rue Notre-Dame-des- Champs*, 1887: p.17, *Monet in his studio at Giverny*, 1921: p.22, *The Villa des Brillants, Meudon*: p.31, *Rodin's desk at the Hôtel Biron*, ca.1908: p.23, *Rodin photographed by Nadar*, 1893: p.31

Acknowledgments: Mathilde Manche, Julie Brousmiche and everyone involved in the production of this book.

Did you enjoy this book?
Find all our books in our online shop

www.kateart.com